For Helen, Mark, and all the family
M. M.

For Mike, Mum, Dad, and Alex
K. H.

ROBIN MIGRATION FACTS

• Robins and their nests may be signs of spring in North America, but in Britain, the small, bright red Scandinavian robin is associated with Christmastime. They begin looking for a mate just before Christmas, and by mid-January, most will have found one.

• The Scandinavian robins migrate to Britain in the winter to escape the harsher northern winters and because it is easier for them to find food. Their epic migratory journey across Europe can take from three days to a full week.

• Migrating robins use the stars to navigate, and can fly up to 1,600 feet above the ground or sea level. If the sky is too cloudy, they will stop and wait until they can see the stars again before continuing their journey.

COMING HOME
is a DAVID FICKLING BOOK published in partnership with WAITROSE

First published in Great Britain in 2016 by
David Fickling Books, 31 Beaumont Street, Oxford, OX1 2NP
www.davidficklingbooks.com

Coming Home was inspired by the Waitrose Christmas television advertisement, 2016
Text copyright © 2016 by Michael Morpurgo
Illustrations copyright © 2016 by Kerry Hyndman

First U.S. edition 2018

Library of Congress Catalog Card Number pending
ISBN 978-1-5362-0042-3

18 19 20 21 22 23 TLF 10 9 8 7 6 5 4 3 2 1

Printed in Dongguan, Guangdong, China

This book was typeset in Bell MT.
The illustrations were created digitally.

Candlewick Press
99 Dover Street
Somerville, Massachusetts 02144

visit us at www.candlewick.com

COMING
HOME

MICHAEL MORPURGO
illustrated by KERRY HYNDMAN

CANDLEWICK PRESS

Come, my heart, and come, my wings,
Fly, fly before the cruel snows,
Carry me, carry me home.
I must be on my way.
On my way.

Safe in the shadows, safe among trees.
Darting, flitting, swooping, and soaring,
Onward, upward, long way to go.
Get there I must, get there I will. I will.

Out of the forest, into the daylight,
Over the fields, follow the valleys,
Find the river, my river will guide me.
Be strong, my wings, beat fast,
Beat on.

Dream of home, think only of her,
Waiting for me, looking for me, longing for me.
Beat, my wings, beat faster.
Easy, my heart, go steady.
Steady.

Dark clouds gather over mountain peaks.
A rumble and roaring of thunder.
Lightning flashes and crackles.
A hard, hard rain batters me down,
Down.

Make for the bank, for a sheltering tree.
Will these weary wings keep me flying?
Heavy my wings and heavy my heart,
Will I ever see my home again?

Lift me, lift me!
Perched here at last!

Safe and sound, from storm and rain.
Let feathers dry, let thunder pass.
Rest, my heart, and rest, my wings,
And sleep.

Wings awake, feathers dry, strong again.
Over the mountains, over the sea,
Long way to fly, no rest there.
One last drink and I'm ready to go.
Ready to go.

Sleep still in my head, I drink deep, drink too long.
Hear the wind of his wings,
The hawk shriek above.
Coming after me, eyes burning,
Talons raking, claws at my neck . . .

Turn, twist,

dart, weave,

dive.

Break free, fly free of him.

Only just.

Take me home, my wings, carry me home.
She's longing for me, looking for me.
Ahead I see great mountain peaks
Above the swirling clouds.
Beat strong, my wings,
Beat strong.

Over the mountains at last.
On I fly through falling snow, driving snow.
A blinding blizzard. Find somewhere to hide, fast.
Must rest, must shelter from the snow,
From the cold.

Here I must wait for the skies to clear, for the wind to calm.
But stay too long and cold will kill.

Then a hush of birds fills the sky,
A flock of thrushes, calling, "Join us! Join us!"

We fly together, sing together, chatter together,
Land in a field to feed. Rest, my wings, my heart.
Each of us on the lookout for each other,
Out over sun-dancing sea,
Homeward bound.

A rolling sea fog ahead, covers us, hides us
From one another, from the sea, from the sky.
Flying blind in a world of white,
Lost and quite alone.
How high? How low?
Where am I?

I am

spinning,

tumbling,

falling.

Lift, my wings, take sudden flight.
Dart through surf, claws skimming the sea,
This raging sea below me.
A wide wild sea still to cross. Tired now,
So tired.

Then, below me, a blessed boat.
A blessed, beautiful bobbing boat!
A home for me on the wild wide sea.
Down I go.

The deck pitches and rocks, rises and falls.
   Judge the landing, get it just right.

Perch, cling on, but a breaking wave sweeps me away,

Down onto the deck, rolls me over and over.
Helpless now.

Until, until . . .

I look up and see

One big boot,
then two big hands,
reaching for me,

Then nothing.

Waking from my dreams, dreams of her, of home.
Warm all through, my feathers dry.

Easy to be happy here.
They give me drink, and raisins.
I grow strong again, ready to go,
Must go.

Flutter to the window, flutter to the door.
They know I have to go. Cupped in kindest hands,
"Off you go, little bird, off you go!"
Waved away, cheered away,
heart full of thanks.
On my way.
I'm coming home.

And I know my way too,
Feel it in my bones,
In my wings, in my heart.
A shining sea below me,
Calmer waters, sandy shores,
crying gulls.

Farms and fields below me now.
Homeland, but not home. Not yet.

Will she be there, will she be waiting?
To see her, be with her, is all I long for,
All I have flown for. Not far now.

Bring me home, my beating wings,
Bring me home, my beating heart.

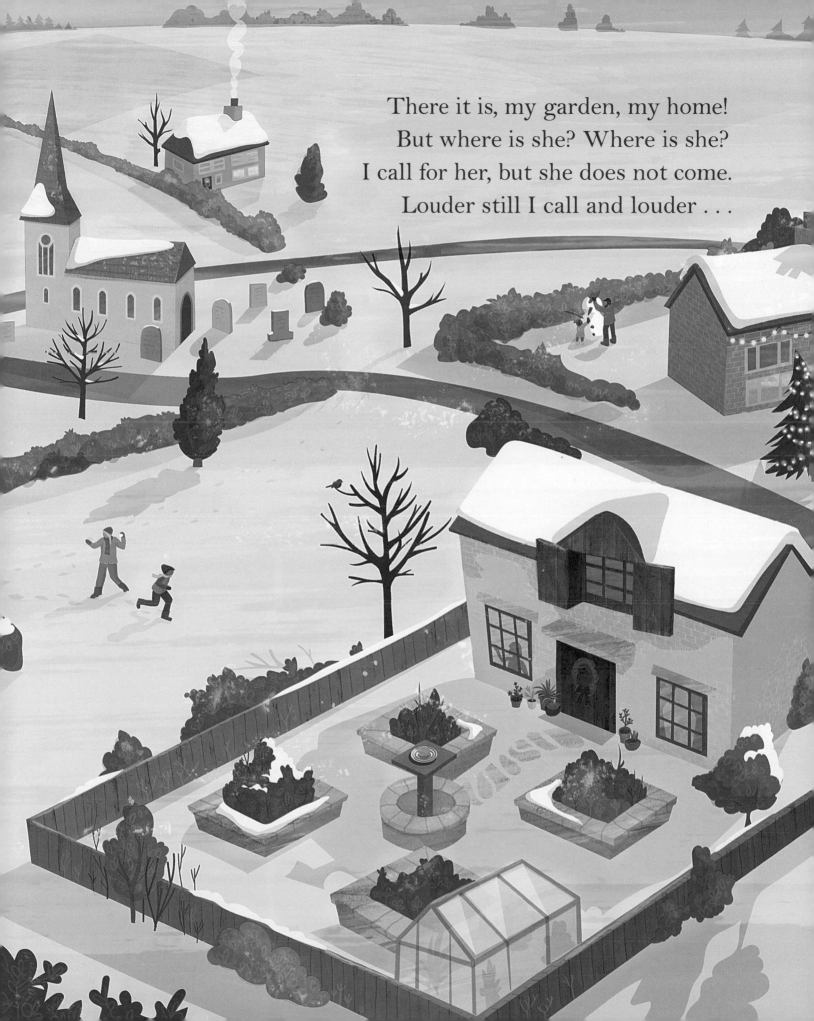

There it is, my garden, my home!
But where is she? Where is she?
I call for her, but she does not come.
Louder still I call and louder . . .

and there she comes.
At last, at last.

"What kept you?" she asks me.
"Oh, this and that," I tell her.
"This and that."

"Look at the window," she says.
"Our very best friend. She's been waiting too.
We've all been waiting."

The window opens. "What kept you? I've been worried sick. He's home! The robin. They're together again. Eating my Christmas bird cake. Come look, Mom! Come see, Dad!

I can have a merry Christmas now.
We can *all* have a merry Christmas now."